THE LION SLEEPS TONIGHT

JULIA WILLIAMSON

The Lion Sleeps Tonight by Julia Williamson

ISBN 978-1-387-22582-8

THE LION SLEEPS TONIGHT

JULIA WILLIAMSON

90
20
36
42
51
7
16
5
4
10
½

In the not-so-quiet jungle
Marcello can not sleep.

The thunderous snore
Of a pack of boars
Scared off his counting sheep.

He went to count the zebras
By the waterhole instead,

But when they saw him coming
They all turned their tails and fled!

Marcello tried counting antelope,
Standing together in a pack.

But like the zebras they took off!
Not one of them looked back.

Marcello found a herd of elephants.
Surely, they would not be afraid.

But he found he could not sleep
With all the ruckus noise they made.

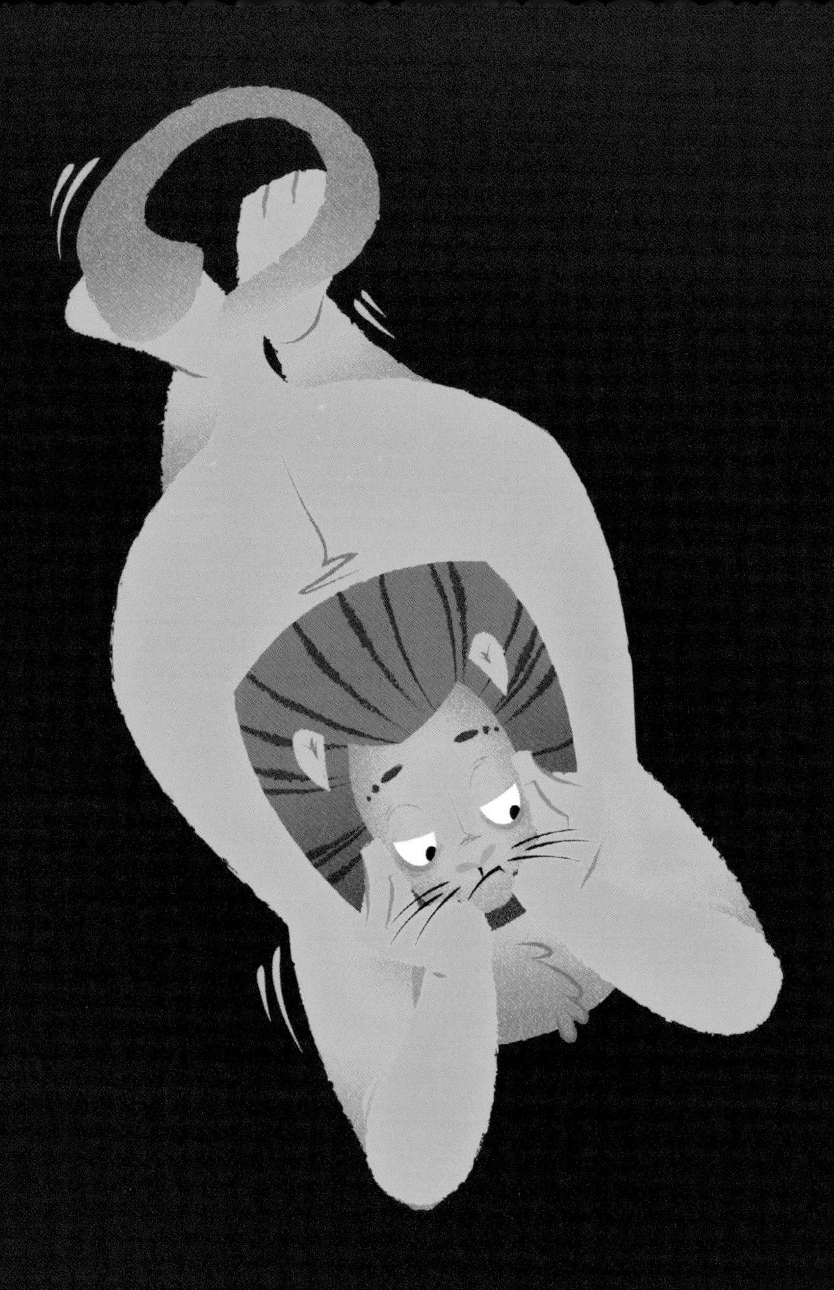

Marcello tried counting fire ants
Marching softly through the night.

But he was soon awakened
Covered with their stingy bites.

One day he tried to climb high up
Into the canopy

To try to nap just like the panther
Sleeping in the trees.

He used his claws to climb up high
But soon he quickly found

That some big cats are better suited
Sleeping on the ground.

If by chance
He might have thought
That shut-eye was in reach,

Some silly bird
High up above
Would wake him with a

EEECCCHHH!!!!

One night Marcello came upon
A clearing in the trees.

He thought that this might me be the place
To help him snooze with ease.

He thought this place was perfect,
But surprisingly he found,

That he couldn’t fall asleep
If no one else was around.

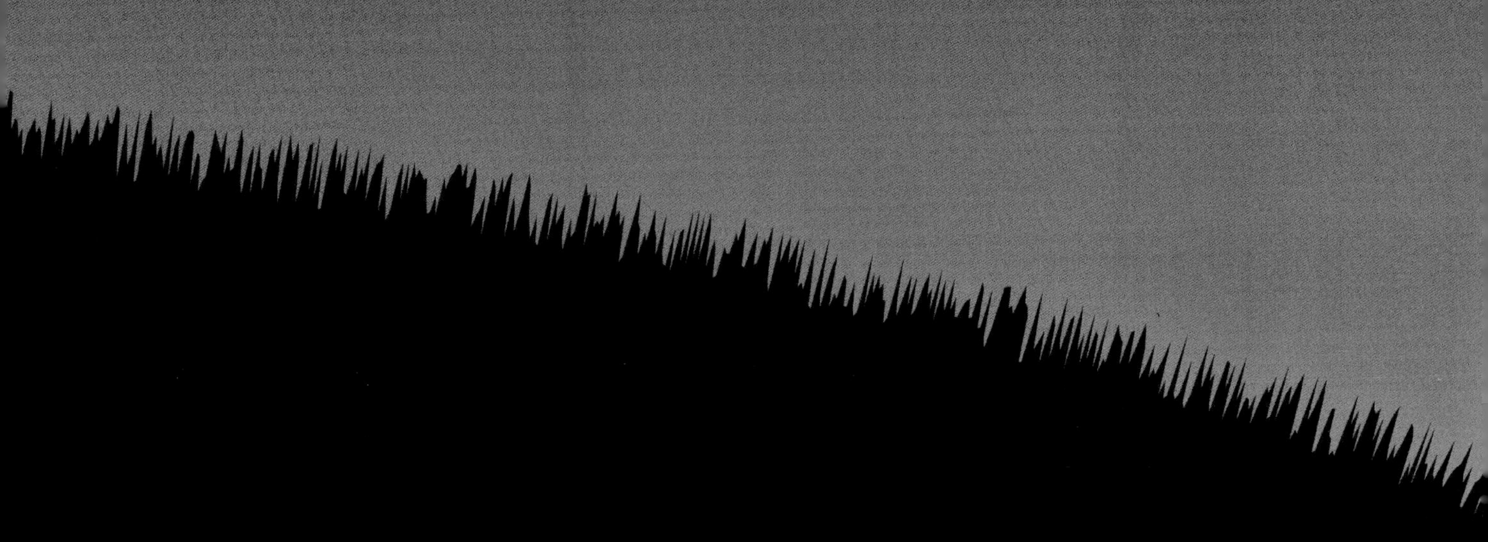

He missed all the commotion.
He missed the wild boars' snore.

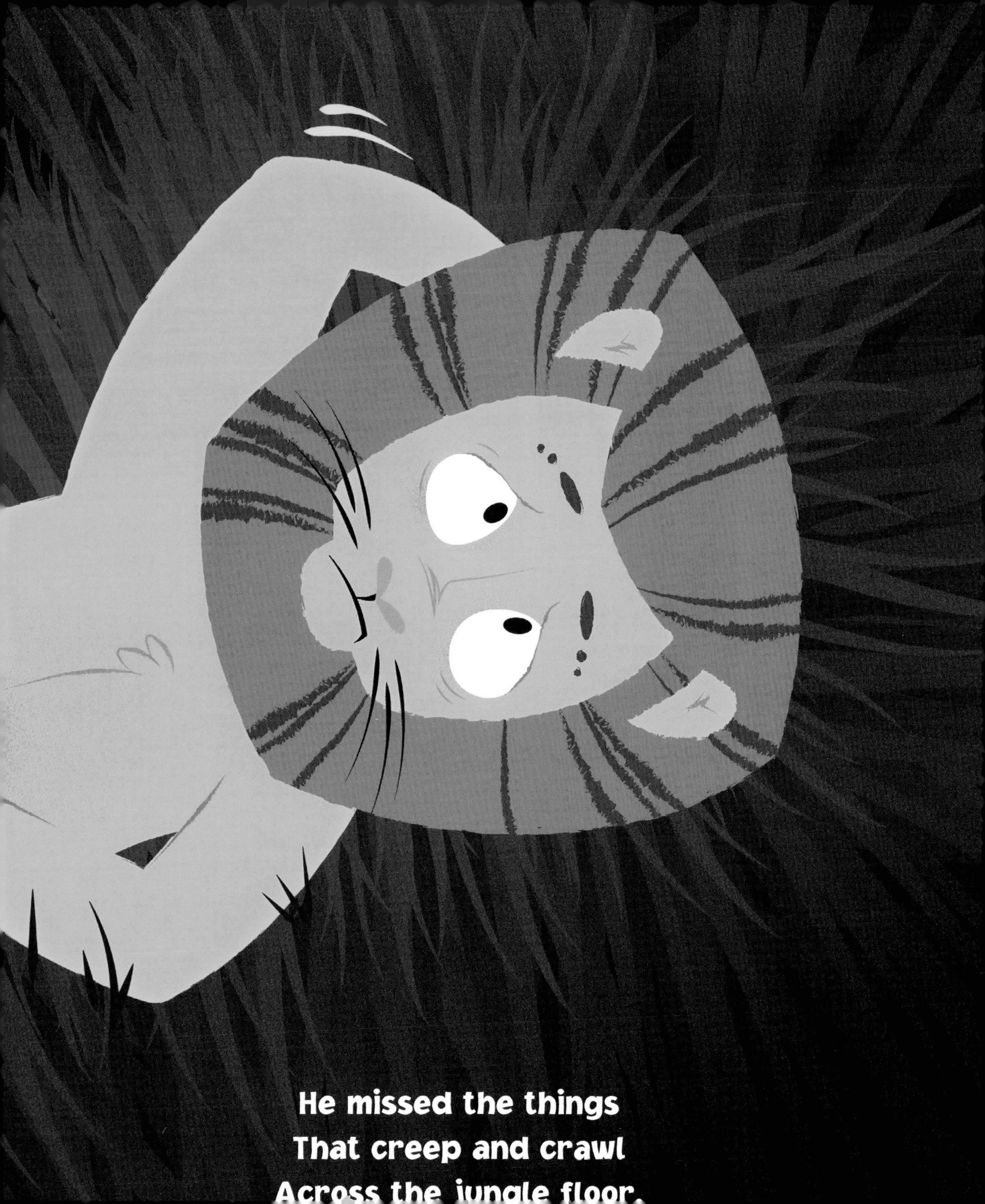

He missed the things
That creep and crawl
Across the jungle floor.

He missed the herd of elephants.
In fact, they really were alright!

In the not-so-quiet jungle
He missed the creatures of the night.

Marcello missed the jungle.
So quickly he returned.

And he never EVER forgot about
The lesson he had learned.

For the first time in forever
With his sleepy eyes closed,

Marcello slept all night
Until the morning sun rose.

7
8
15
16
1
22